se you

e Cross

strated by

Chamberlain

Bananas

It was one of those bad days.

Kitty never knew how they began.

Everything was

going wrong.

5

Dad said Kitty must have

got out of bed the wrong side.

She didn't want to do anything, and she

lost things, and nothing seemed fair.

Mum and Dad took no notice.

'Why aren't they worrying about me?'

she asked her brother Dan.

Dan said, 'They're in a good mood – but

you wouldn't understand that, Kitty.'

'Why not?' asked Kitty.

Dan laughed and said, 'Because you
don't know what a good mood is!'

He stuck his tongue out
at her and ran away.

Kitty had been cross before but now she was very, very cross. She chased her brother down the stairs . . .

. . . and out of the kitchen . . .

. . . and along the hall.

But he was too quick for her,

and slipped out through the front door.

Kitty stomped into the living room, slamming the door behind her. And that was when it started.

SLAM

She slammed the door so hard it made

the room shake . . .

. . . and Mum's lovely old

jug on the table fell over

and broke into three pieces.

Worse than that, it fell

against Sandy's cage,

which was right at the

edge of the table.

The door flew open, and the terrified

hamster scuttled out across the carpet.

Kitty dived down to catch her.

But Sandy slipped

through her hands like

a bar of

wet soap.

Sandy ran fast and

Kitty chased her,

knocking over ornaments

and photographs . . .

. . . and the wastepaper basket which

scattered rubbish all over the floor.

Kitty got on her hands and knees and

saw Sandy disappear behind the sofa.

Kitty knew she had to catch Sandy before she went down the hole in the skirting board and was lost forever! Quickly, she pulled off all the cushions.

Then she piled them at one end of the

sofa so Sandy couldn't get out.

Then, puffing and blowing, she pulled
the sofa away from the wall.

But the sofa knocked over the lamp . . .

. . . which knocked over a vase of flowers . . .

. . . and all the water poured

over the rug.

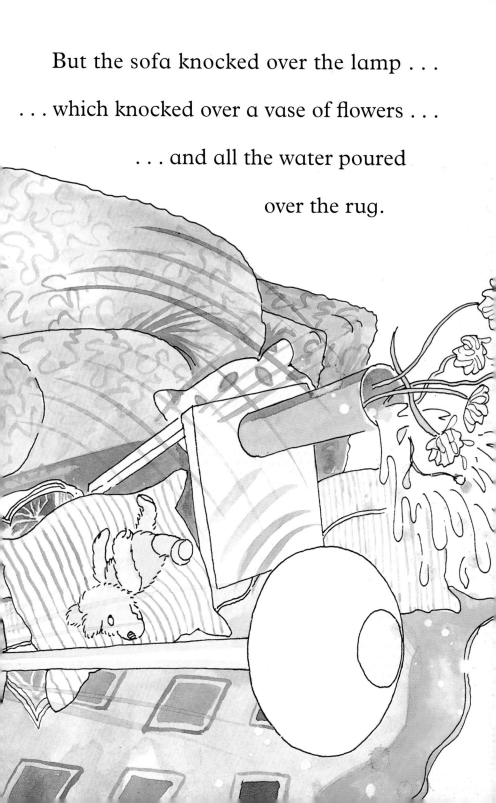

Suddenly Kitty spotted Sandy. She made a last grab, and caught her tightly in her hand.

She put Sandy safely back in her

cage and closed the door.

Then Kitty looked around and saw what she had done. There was stuff all over the place, and a wet patch on the rug.

It was terrible!

She heard Mum and
Dad come in the kitchen
door from the garden.

Two minutes later she went into the

kitchen smiling sweetly.

Mum handed Kitty a drink

and a chocolate biscuit.

'When we've had a drink, we're going to put some plants in the garden. Want to help, Kitty?' Mum said.

Kitty nodded and said, 'Oh, Mum, I'd love to.' Now Kitty hated gardening and Mum and Dad knew that. They gave each other a funny look.

Kitty knew she had to tell them what had happened in the living room, but she didn't know how to begin. So she said, 'I think you're the best parents in the world.'

Her mum and dad gave each other another funny look.

At last Kitty blurted out: 'If I tell you something, do you promise you won't be cross?' Her mum and dad promised.

Slowly, Kitty led them to the living room.

At the door she stopped.

'Sandy escaped, and I made a bit of a

mess in the living room trying to catch

her,' said Kitty.

Mum and Dad laughed.

Just a very little mess.

They opened the living room door.

Kitty stood well back.

Mum's face changed.

Kitty went backwards down the hall.

'Come here, Kitty!' Dad called. 'Do you
call this a little mess!'

'How could you let this happen?' asked

Mum. She sounded really upset.

'But you promised you wouldn't be cross,' said Kitty, almost in tears.

'OK, OK,' said Dad, 'but now it's your turn to promise us something.'

Kitty agreed.

'Right then,' said Dad, '*You tidy the room.*'

Kitty groaned.

Kitty knew she had to start tidying. But

she gave Sandy a cross look.

It took a long time to put everything in order. It was very hard work. Dan came to help, and tried to glue Mum's jug.

At last the room looked better.

And Kitty found out that when

you tidy up, you sometimes come across

things you thought you'd lost.

Kitty ran into the garden to show Mum and Dad the plaster model kit she'd got for her birthday.

'Look – now I'm going to make you a lovely present, Mum – to make up for what I did to the living room,' she said.

Mum smiled. 'Oh, Kit – does that mean you're going to make another mess?'

'I'll try not to,' Kitty said,

'but if I do . . .'

'Promise you won't be cross!'